CIDER AND SHUTTER

CIDER AND SHUTTER

COZY AUTUMN ROMANCE

ANN LAUREL

Truth is stranger than fiction, but it is because Fiction is obliged to stick to possibilities; Truth isn't.

— MARK TWAIN

CHAPTER ONE

*R*akel

    I fumbled with the display easel, my fingers trembling as I tried to secure my best autumn landscape print. The bustling energy of the Maple Grove Farmers Market swirled around me, a cacophony of voices and aromas that only heightened my nerves. I'd been here for an hour already, and not a single person had stopped to look at my photographs.

"Deep breaths, Rakel," I muttered to myself, adjusting the framed print for the umpteenth time. "You've got this."

But did I? The doubt crept in, insidious as the morning mist that often shrouded the countryside I loved to capture through my lens. I glanced around at the other booths with vibrant displays of fresh produce, homemade jams, and artisanal crafts. My little corner of the market felt painfully out of place, a testament to my struggle to find my footing in this tight-knit community.

I reached for my vintage Nikon, the familiar weight of it in my hands a small comfort. Through my viewfinder, the world always made more sense. I focused on a nearby stall, where an elderly woman was carefully arranging a basket of apples. Click. The shutter captured the moment of her weathered hands, the glossy red skin of the fruit, the interplay of light and shadow.

"Now that's a keeper," a deep voice said from behind me.

I spun around, nearly dropping my camera in surprise. A tall man stood there, his warm brown eyes crinkling at the corners, as he smiled. He was the epitome of small-town charm in his worn jeans and flannel shirt, sleeves rolled up to reveal tanned, muscular forearms.

"I... thank you," I stammered, feeling heat rise to my cheeks. "I'm Rakel. Rakel Boswell."

"Tevin Short," he replied, extending a hand. He was mighty attractive. I pushed the thought aside, reminding myself I was here to promote my business, not daydream about handsome strangers.

Tevin's gaze swept over my display, lingering on each photograph. "These are incredible," he said, gesturing to a series of shots capturing the changing colors of Maple Grove's famous sugar maples. "You've really got an eye for the subtleties of the season."

My chest swelled with pride, even as my inner critic tried to dismiss his praise. "That's very kind of you to say," I managed, tucking a stray curl behind my ear. "I've always loved autumn in Maple Grove. There's something magical about the way the light filters through the trees this time of year."

"I couldn't agree more," Tevin nodded, his expression thoughtful. "Do you specialize in nature photography?"

And just like that, the floodgates opened. I explained my techniques, my inspiration, the way I sought to capture not just the visual beauty of a scene, but the feeling it evoked. Tevin listened intently, asking insightful questions that revealed a genuine interest in my work.

As we talked, I felt myself relaxing, the knot of anxiety in my stomach slowly unraveling. For the first time in months, I felt truly seen and appreciated for my art. It was intoxicating.

"So, how long have you been doing this professionally?" Tevin asked, leaning against the edge of my booth.

I hesitated, biting my lower lip. "Well, I opened my studio about a year ago, but..." I trailed off, unsure how to admit that my dream was teetering on the edge of failure.

Tevin's expression softened, understanding dawning in his eyes. "It's not easy, is it? Starting a business in a small town?"

I shook my head, feeling a lump form in my throat. "Sometimes I wonder if I'm cut out for this," I confessed, the words tumbling out before I could stop them. "If maybe I should have listened to my parents and pursued something more practical."

"Hey now," Tevin said gently, his hand coming to rest on my arm. The touch was brief, but comforting. "From what I can see, you absolutely are cut out for this. You just need the right opportunity to showcase your talent."

His words wrapped around me like a warm blanket, soothing the raw edges of my self-doubt. I offered him a small, grateful smile. "Thank you," I said softly. "I think I needed to hear that more than I realized."

As if on cue, a small group of people approached my booth, drawn in by our conversation. I straightened up, switching into what I called my *professional mode*, as I explained my work to the potential customers. To my surprise and delight, I sold two prints and booked a family portrait session.

When the group moved on, I turned back to Tevin,

practically buzzing with excitement. "I can't believe it! That's more business than I've had in weeks!"

Tevin's smile was warm and genuine. "See? I told you. You've got real talent, Rakel. You just need to believe in yourself a little more."

As the morning wore on, Tevin stayed close to my booth, chatting with me between customers. I learned he owned the local apple orchard, a fact that immediately set my photographer's mind racing with ideas for potential shoots.

"You should come out to the orchard sometime," Tevin suggested, as if reading my thoughts. "The trees are just starting to turn. It'd make for some beautiful shots."

"I'd love that," I replied, trying to keep the eagerness out of my voice. "Maybe we could discuss some sort of collaboration? I've been thinking about doing a series on local businesses, capturing the heart of Maple Grove, you know?"

Tevin's eyes lit up. "That sounds fantastic. I'm always looking for new ways to promote the orchard. And who knows? Maybe we could set up a little display of your work in our farm store."

The possibility made my heart soar. This could be exactly the break I needed. But before I could respond, a commotion at the far end of the market caught our attention.

"Oh no," Tevin muttered, his brow furrowing. "Looks like Old Man Guthrie's up to his usual tricks."

I followed his gaze to see an elderly man in overalls gesticulating wildly at a group of confused-looking tourists. His booming voice carried across the market. "You city folk don't know nothin' about real produce! These here toma-toes are worth their weight in gold, I tell ya!"

Tevin sighed, running a hand through his hair. "I should

probably go handle this. Guthrie means well, but he can get a bit overzealous with the out-of-towners."

I nodded, trying to hide my disappointment at his imminent departure. "Of course. Go ahead. It was really nice meeting you, Tevin."

He hesitated for a moment, then reached into his pocket. "Actually, do you have a business card? I'd love to follow up about that orchard shoot. And, well..." he trailed off, a hint of color rising to his cheeks. "Maybe we could grab coffee sometime? To discuss business, of course."

My heart did a little flip as I fumbled in my bag for a card. "Y-yes, of course," I stammered, producing a slightly bent card. As I handed it to him, our fingers brushed, and I felt the same spark from earlier.

Tevin tucked the card into his shirt pocket, patting it as if to keep it safe. "I have a feeling we'll be seeing each other again soon, Rakel Boswell," he said with a wink before turning to deal with the Guthrie situation.

As I watched him go, I felt a flutter of excitement in my chest. For the first time in a long while, I felt hopeful about the future both for my business and for something I couldn't quite name yet.

The rest of the market day passed in a blur of customers and conversations. By the time I started packing up my booth, I had sold several more prints and booked two more portrait sessions. It was more success than I'd had in months, and I couldn't help but feel that meeting Tevin had somehow shifted my luck.

As I carefully placed my framed photographs back into their protective cases, I overheard snippets of conversation from nearby vendors.

"Did you see Tevin Short chatting up the new photographer girl?" a woman's voice said, tinged with curiosity.

"About time that boy showed interest in someone,"

another replied. "Lord knows his mama's been trying to set him up for years."

I felt my cheeks burn, half embarrassed, and half intrigued by their gossip. I hadn't realized Tevin was such a subject of local interest. Then again, as the owner of one of the town's biggest attractions, I supposed it made sense.

I was so lost in thought that I nearly jumped out of my skin when someone tapped me on the shoulder. I turned to find myself face-to-face with the elderly woman I had photographed earlier, the one arranging apples when Tevin first approached.

"Excuse me, dear," she said, her voice warm and slightly raspy. "I couldn't help but notice you taking my picture earlier. Normally, I'd be a bit put out, but your young man seemed mighty impressed by it."

"Oh, he's not my—" I protested, but she waved me off with a knowing smile.

"Now, now, no need to be shy. I'm Mabel Guthrie, by the way. You must be new in town?"

I nodded, introducing myself properly. As we chatted, I learned Mabel was Old Man Guthrie's wife and a fixture at the farmer's market for over fifty years.

"Listen, honey," she said, leaning in conspiratorially. "I've got a proposition for you. How would you like to do a little project on the history of our market? We're coming up on our centennial next year, and the committee's been looking for someone to put together a photo display for the celebration."

My eyes widened at the opportunity. "That sounds amazing, Mrs. Guthrie. I'd be honored to be considered."

Mabel patted my hand. "Consider yourself more than considered, dear. I'll put in a good word with the rest of the old biddies on the committee." She winked. "And who knows? Maybe you'll need to get some historical context from that nice Tevin Short. His family's orchard has been part of this market since the beginning, you know."

As Mabel walked away, leaving me with her contact information and a promise to be in touch, I felt like I was walking on air. In one market day, I'd gone from feeling like an outsider to potentially landing a major local project.

I finished packing up my booth, my mind racing with ideas for the centennial project. As I loaded the last box into my beat-up Subaru, I caught sight of Tevin across the parking lot. He was helping an elderly couple load their car with purchases, his sweet smile visible even from a distance.

As if sensing my gaze, he looked up, catching my eye. He raised a hand in a wave, and I returned the gesture, feeling a warmth spread through my chest that had nothing to do with the autumn sun.

Driving home to my small apartment above my studio, I couldn't stop smiling. For the first time since I'd moved to Maple Grove and opened my business, I felt like I was exactly where I was meant to be. The day had been full of unexpected connections and opportunities, and I couldn't wait to see where they might lead.

As I unlocked the door to my apartment, my phone buzzed with a text from an unknown number:

Hope your first market was a success. Looking forward to that orchard shoot. Coffee this week to discuss? - Tevin

I bit my lip, trying to contain my grin as I typed out a reply. Maybe things were finally falling into place. As I set my camera bag down and collapsed onto my worn couch, I allowed myself a moment of pure, unadulterated hope.

Tomorrow, I'd wake up early, head to my tiny studio downstairs, and start planning for the centennial project. But for now, I closed my eyes, letting the events of the day wash over me. The scent of apples and cinnamon still lingered in my nostrils, mingling with the earthy aroma of fresh produce and the inexplicable excitement of new beginnings.

At that moment, I felt like I could capture it all in a single, perfect photograph with the essence of Maple Grove, of autumn, of possibility. And for once, the voice of self-doubt that usually whispered in the back of my mind was blessedly, wonderfully silent.

CHAPTER TWO

*T*evin

I wiped the sweat from my brow as I loaded the last crate of apples onto my truck. The orchard was alive with the sounds of harvest, with ladders creaking, apples thudding into baskets, and the cheerful chatter of my workers. It was a good year for the Short family orchard, but I couldn't shake the feeling that something was missing.

As I climbed into the driver's seat, I noticed a small package on the passenger side. "Ah man," I muttered, realizing I'd forgotten to deliver it earlier. I glanced at the address label and did a double-take. Rakel Boswell Photography Studio. My heart skipped a beat as I remembered the captivating photographer I'd met at the farmer's market last week.

Before I knew it, I was parking outside her studio in downtown Maple Grove. I sat there for a moment, package in hand, suddenly feeling nervous. "Get it together, Tevin," I chided myself. "You're just delivering a package."

The bell above the door chimed as I entered. The

studio was smaller than I expected, but it exuded warmth and creativity. Photographs of autumn scenes lined the walls, each one capturing the essence of the season in a way that took my breath away.

"Hello?" Rakel's soft voice called from the back room. She appeared a moment later, her curly auburn hair pulled back in a messy bun. A smudge of ink on her cheek made her look endearingly disheveled. "Tevin? What are you doing here?"

I held up the package, suddenly feeling foolish. "I, uh, I had a delivery mix-up. This accidentally went to the address next door, but I thought I'd drop it off personally."

Rakel's hazel eyes lit up with amusement. "You came all the way here to deliver my package to my neighbor?"

I felt the heat rise in my cheeks. "Well, when you put it that way, it does sound a bit ridiculous."

She laughed, a sound that made me want to hear it again and again. "It's not ridiculous. It's sweet."

As we chatted, I opened up about the orchard, my family's legacy, and the pressure I felt to keep it all going. Rakel listened intently, her eyes full of understanding.

"It sounds like you have a lot on your shoulders," she said softly.

I nodded, surprised at how easy it was to talk to her. "Sometimes I wonder if I'm doing the right thing, you know? Carrying on the family business when part of me wants to try something new."

Rakel bit her lower lip, a gesture I found incredibly endearing. "Maybe there's a way to do both? Honor your family's legacy while also pursuing your own passions?"

Her words struck a chord in me. I looked around her studio, taking in the beautiful photographs, and suddenly had an idea. "You know, the orchard could use some professional photos for marketing. And I've been thinking about hosting events..."

Rakel's eyes widened with interest. "That could be amazing! I've always wanted to do a photoshoot in an orchard."

As we bounced ideas back and forth, a spark of excitement bubbled forth I hadn't experienced in years. Here was someone who understood the balance between tradition and innovation, someone who saw the beauty in what I'd always taken for granted.

"So, tell me more about your work," I said, genuinely curious. "How did you get into photography?"

Rakel's face lit up, and she led me deeper into her studio. "It all started when I was a kid, actually. My grandfather gave me his old camera, and I just fell in love with capturing moments."

As she spoke, I noticed a series of black and white portraits on one wall. They were striking, with each face seemed to tell a story, revealing something raw and honest about the subject.

"These are incredible," I murmured, stepping closer to examine them.

Rakel blushed slightly. "Thanks. That's a personal project I've been working on. Portraits of the *unseen* people in our community. The ones who keep things running but often go unnoticed."

I recognized a few faces as the woman who ran the local diner, the janitor at the elementary school, the guy who delivered mail on the outskirts of town. Seeing them through Rakel's lens made me appreciate them in a whole new way.

"You have a real gift," I said, turning to face her. "You don't just take pictures. You tell stories."

Her smile was shy but pleased. "That's exactly what I'm

trying to do. I want my photos to make people feel something, you know?"

I nodded, thinking about how her images of the orchard could tell the story of my family's legacy in a way words never could. "I definitely know what you mean."

As we continued to talk, I looked at a small workbench in the corner. Various tools and what looked like half-finished projects cluttered the small workbench.

"What's all this?" I asked, gesturing to the bench.

Rakel's eyes lit up. "Oh, that's my tinkering station. I love experimenting with different techniques and materials."

She picked up what looked like a piece of driftwood, with a photograph somehow transferred onto its surface. "This is a wood transfer I've been working on. I'm trying to merge my photography with more tactile, natural elements."

I ran my fingers over the piece, marveling at how the image seemed to be part of the wood itself. "This is amazing, Rakel. Have you ever thought about selling these?"

She shrugged, looking uncertain. "I've considered it, but I wasn't sure if there'd be a market for them."

"Are you kidding?" I said, perhaps a bit too enthusiastically. "People would love these. You know, we have an old barn at the orchard that we've been thinking about converting into an event space. Something like this would be perfect for decorating it."

Rakel's eyes widened. "Really? You think so?"

I nodded emphatically. "Absolutely. In fact..." I hesitated for a moment, then took the plunge. "Why don't you come out to the orchard sometime this week? You could scout some locations for that photoshoot we talked about, and I could show you the barn. Maybe we could brainstorm some ideas for how to use your work in the space."

Rakel bit her lip again, looking both excited and nervous. "That sounds wonderful, Tevin. But are you sure? I don't want to impose or get in the way of your work."

I waved off her concern. "Trust me, it's no imposition at all. In fact, I'm looking forward to it. How about Wednesday afternoon? The light is usually perfect for photos around that time."

She nodded, a smile spreading across her face. "Wednesday sounds perfect. I can't wait to see the orchard."

As I prepared to leave, I found myself reluctant to go. There was something about Rakel's presence that made me feel both energized and at ease. It was a combination I wasn't used to, but one I definitely wanted to experience again.

"Oh, before I forget," I said, reaching into my pocket. "I brought you something." I pulled out a small paper bag and handed it to her.

Rakel opened it curiously, her face lighting up as she saw what was inside. "Apples!"

I grinned. "Not just any apples. These are from our experimental plot. We're trying out some new heirloom varieties. I thought you might like to taste them."

She immediately pulled one out and took a bite, her eyes closing in appreciation. "Oh my god, Tevin. This is amazing. What variety is this?"

"That's a Crimson Crisp," I said, feeling a surge of pride. "It's a newer variety, but it's quickly becoming one of my favorites."

Rakel took another bite, savoring it. "I can see why. The flavor is incredible."

As she enjoyed the apple, I studied her face, noticing the way her freckles danced across her nose and cheeks, the slight dimple that appeared when she smiled. I realized I was staring and quickly looked away, clearing my throat.

"Well, I should probably get going," I said reluctantly. "Got to finish up those deliveries."

Rakel nodded, walking me to the door. "Of course. Thank you for stopping by, Tevin. And for the apples. I'm really looking forward to Wednesday."

"Me too," I said, meaning it more than I'd expected to. As I stepped out onto the sidewalk, I turned back to her. "Oh, and Rakel? Don't forget to bring your camera to the orchard. I have a feeling you're going to find plenty of inspiration there."

Her smile was radiant as she waved goodbye. As I walked back to my truck, I couldn't help but feel like something had shifted. The day suddenly seemed brighter, full of possibilities I hadn't considered before.

Climbing into the driver's seat, I caught sight of my reflection in the rearview mirror. I was grinning like an idiot. "Pull yourself together, Short," I muttered, but I couldn't wipe the smile off my face.

As I drove back towards the orchard, my mind was racing with ideas. The barn renovation, the photo shoot, Rakel's wood transfers, and suddenly, the future of the orchard seemed full of exciting possibilities. And if I was being honest with myself, it wasn't just the business prospects that had me feeling this way.

I looked forward to Wednesday with an anticipation I hadn't felt in years. There was something about Rakel that brought out a side of me I'd almost forgotten existed of a side that dreamed, that created, that saw beauty in the everyday moments of life.

As I pulled up to the orchard, I saw my sister, Liv, waiting by the barn. Liv stood by the barn, her arms crossed, and that look on her face that usually meant I was in for a lecture.

"Where have you been?" she demanded as I got out of the truck. "We've got a ton of work to do, and you just disappear for hours?"

I held up my hands in surrender. "Sorry, Liv. I had to make a delivery in town. It took longer than I expected."

She raised an eyebrow, clearly not buying it. "A delivery? Since when do you handle deliveries personally?"

I busied myself with unloading the empty crates from the truck, avoiding her gaze. "Since now, I guess. Look, I'm sorry I was gone so long. What do you need help with?"

Liv sighed, her annoyance fading into concern. "Tevin, what's going on with you lately? You've been distracted, disappearing at odd times. Is everything okay?"

I paused, considering how to answer. Liv and I had always been close, but lately, it felt like we were drifting apart. She was so focused on running the orchard exactly as our parents had, while I... Well, I wasn't sure what I wanted anymore.

"Everything's fine," I said finally. "I've just been thinking about some new ideas for the orchard. Actually, I wanted to talk to you about that. What would you think about renovating the old barn into an event space?"

Liv's eyes widened in surprise. "An event space? What for?"

I shrugged, trying to sound casual. "Weddings, corporate retreats, that sort of thing. It could bring in some extra revenue, especially during the off-season."

My sister looked skeptical. "I don't know. That sounds like a lot of work and expense. And it's not really what we do here."

"Maybe it's time we branched out a bit," I suggested.

"The orchard's been in our family for generations, but that doesn't mean we can't try new things."

Liv studied me for a moment, her expression unreadable. "This isn't just about the barn, is it? What's really going on, Tevin?"

I sighed, leaning against the truck. "I've been thinking a lot lately about the future of the orchard. About my future. I love this place, Liv, you know I do. But sometimes I wonder if there's more we could be doing, you know?"

My sister's face softened. "Is this about that photographer girl? The one from the farmers market?"

I felt my cheeks heat up. "Rakel? No, it's not... I mean, she's part of it, I guess. She just sees things differently. It's made me start to look at the orchard in a new way."

Liv was quiet for a moment, then she surprised me by pulling me into a hug. "You've always been the dreamer in the family. I should have known you'd get restless eventually."

I hugged her back, feeling a rush of affection for my stubborn, practical sister. "I'm not restless, exactly. I just think maybe it's time for some changes around here."

She pulled back, giving me a wry smile. "Changes, huh? Like inviting a certain auburn-haired photographer out to the orchard?"

I groaned. "How did you know about that?"

Liv laughed. "Small town, remember? Nothing stays secret for long. Plus, I may have overheard you on the phone earlier."

I shook my head, chuckling despite my embarrassment. "Alright, alright. Yes, Rakel's coming out here on Wednesday. To take some photos," I added quickly. "For marketing purposes."

"Uh-huh," Liv said, clearly unconvinced. "Well, I think

it's a great idea. The photos, I mean. And maybe some of your other ideas aren't so crazy either."

I raised an eyebrow. "Really? You're okay with all this?"

She shrugged. "I'm not saying yes to anything yet. But I'm willing to listen. Why don't you put together some concrete plans for this event space idea? We can discuss it at the family meeting next week."

I grinned, feeling a weight lift off my shoulders. "Thanks, Liv. I really appreciate that."

As we walked towards the orchard to check on the day's harvest, Liv nudged me with her elbow. "So, this Rakel must be pretty special to get you all worked up like this."

I rolled my eyes, but I couldn't hide my smile. "She's different. In a good way. I don't know, Liv. There's just something about her."

My sister nodded sagely. "Well, I look forward to meeting her. And Tevin? It's nice to see you excited about something again."

As we reached the orchard, the sweet scent of apples filled the air. The late afternoon sun filtered through the trees, casting a golden glow over everything. I took a deep breath, feeling a sense of peace wash over me.

CHAPTER THREE

*R*akel

I gasped as I stepped out of my beat-up Subaru, the beauty of Tevin's family orchard hitting me like a wave. The late afternoon sun filtered through the trees, casting a golden glow over rows upon rows of apple trees laden with ripe fruit. The air was crisp and sweet, carrying the unmistakable scent of autumn.

"Wow," I breathed, fumbling for my camera. I had to capture this magical light, the way it danced across the leaves and apples, creating a tapestry of warm hues.

"I take it, you approve?" Tevin's voice, tinged with amusement, came from behind me.

I spun around, feeling a blush creep up my cheeks. He stood there, looking every bit the rugged orchard owner in his worn jeans and flannel shirt, a gentle smile playing on his lips.

"Tevin! I... yes, it's absolutely breathtaking," I managed, trying to regain my composure. "I can't believe I've lived in Maple Grove for over a year and never saw this place."

He chuckled, stepping closer. "Well, we're a bit off the

beaten path. But I'm glad you're here now." His eyes met mine, and for a moment, I forgot how to breathe. "Ready for the grand tour?"

I nodded eagerly, clutching my camera like a lifeline. "Lead the way!"

As we walked between the rows of trees, Tevin pointed out different varieties of apples, explaining their unique characteristics and flavors. The orchard captivated me, along with the passion in his voice as he spoke about his family's legacy.

"This section here," he said, gesturing to a small grove of gnarled trees, "these are some of the original trees my great-grandfather planted when he first started the orchard."

I raised my camera, framing a shot of the ancient trees against the backdrop of newer, more uniform rows. "That's incredible," I murmured, snapping the photo. "You can almost feel the history here."

Tevin nodded, a hint of pride in his smile. "It's not always easy keeping a place like this going. But moments like this, seeing it through someone else's eyes reminds me why we do it."

I lowered my camera, meeting his gaze. "You should be proud, Tevin. What you have here, it's really special."

He rubbed the back of his neck, looking almost shy. "Thanks, Rakel. That means a lot, coming from you."

We continued our tour, with Tevin showing me the sorting house, where they cleaned and packaged the apples, and the small farm store where they sold fresh produce and homemade goods. All the while, my mind raced with ideas for potential photoshoots with the play of light through the apple trees, close-ups of weathered hands sorting fruit, the rustic charm of the farm store.

As we walked, our conversation flowed easily, punctuated by laughter and shared observations. I opened up to Tevin in a way I hadn't with anyone in a long time, sharing stories of my childhood and my journey to becoming a photographer.

"So, what made you decide to open a studio in Maple Grove?" Tevin asked as we paused by a small pond, its surface reflecting the fiery colors of the surrounding trees.

I bit my lip, considering how to answer. "Honestly? I was running away from a failed relationship and a stalled career in the city. Maple Grove seemed like the perfect place to start over, you know? Small, quiet, beautiful..."

Tevin nodded, his expression understanding. "Sometimes a fresh start is exactly what we need. Though I can't imagine anyone being foolish enough to let you go."

His words sent a warm flutter through my chest, and I quickly raised my camera to hide my flushed cheeks. "Oh look, the light on the water is perfect right now," I said, snapping a few shots of the pond.

Tevin chuckled softly, and I could feel his eyes on me as I worked. When I lowered the camera, he was looking at me with an intensity that made my heart race.

"You know, Rakel," he said, his voice low and earnest, "I'm really glad you came here today. To the orchard, I mean. And to Maple Grove in general."

I swallowed hard, feeling a mix of excitement and nerves. "Me too," I replied softly. "I feel like I'm finally starting to find my place here."

We stood there for a moment, the air between us charged with unspoken possibilities. Then Tevin cleared his throat, gesturing towards a path that led away from the pond.

"There's one more thing I want to show you," he said, a hint of excitement in his voice. "It's my favorite spot on the entire property."

Curious, I followed him down the winding path. As we walked, Tevin told me more about growing up in the orchard, the mischief he and his sister Liv would get into as kids, and the lessons his grandfather taught him about tending to the land.

"He always said that an orchard was more than just trees and fruit," Tevin mused. "It was a living, breathing thing that needed care and respect."

I nodded, understanding completely. "That's how I feel about photography. It's not just about taking pretty pictures. It's about capturing the essence of a moment, the soul of a place or person."

Tevin's eyes lit up. "Exactly! That's what I've been trying to explain to Liv about some changes I want to make around here. It's not about abandoning tradition, it's about finding new ways to honor it."

As we crested a small hill, I gasped. Before us stretched a vista of the entire orchard, the rows of trees creating a patchwork of greens, reds, and golds that seemed to stretch on forever. In the distance, the sun was setting, painting the sky in brilliant hues of orange and pink.

"Oh, Tevin," I breathed, raising my camera with shaking hands. "This is... I don't even have words."

He smiled, a soft, genuine expression that made my heart skip a beat. "I thought you might like it. I come up here sometimes when I need to clear my head or make big decisions. Something about this view always helps put things in perspective."

I snapped photo after photo, trying to capture the majesty of the scene before us. But I knew no image could truly do justice to the feeling of standing there, with the warm breeze rustling through the trees and the golden light bathing everything in its glow.

Lowering my camera, I turned to Tevin. "Thank you for sharing this with me. I can see why it's so special to you."

He nodded, his eyes never leaving mine. "You know, Rakel, I've been thinking... the Maple Grove Fall Festival is coming up next weekend. It's kind of a big deal around here, with hayrides and pumpkin carving and a big bonfire at the end of the night."

I smiled, remembering the posters I'd seen around town advertising the event. "It sounds wonderful. I was thinking of going to take some photos for my portfolio."

Tevin shifted his weight, looking uncharacteristically nervous. "Well, I was wondering... would you maybe want to go together? As friends, of course," he added quickly. "But, you know, it might be nice to have some company while you're taking pictures. And I could introduce you to some folks around town, maybe drum up some business for your studio."

My heart raced at the invitation, even as I tried to temper my excitement. Friends, he had said. But the way he was looking at me, the slight tremor in his voice... it felt like there might be more to it than that.

"I'd love to," I heard myself say, my voice steadier than I felt. "It sounds like fun. And company would be nice."

Tevin's face broke into a wide grin, relief and happiness clear in his expression. "Great! That's... that's really great, Rakel. I'm looking forward to it."

As we stood there, the sun dipping lower on the horizon, a sense of possibility washed over me. This orchard, this town, this man standing beside me... suddenly, it all felt full of promise and potential.

"We should probably head back," Tevin said softly, though he made no move to leave. "It'll be dark soon."

I nodded, but found myself reluctant to leave this

magical spot. "Just one more photo," I said, raising my camera one last time.

But instead of focusing on the landscape, I turned and caught Tevin in profile, his face bathed in the warm glow of the setting sun, a soft smile playing on his lips as he gazed out over his family's land. It was a moment of quiet contentment, of a man perfectly at peace in his element.

As I lowered the camera, Tevin turned to me, eyebrow raised in amusement. "Did you just take a picture of me?"

I felt a blush creep up my cheeks, but met his gaze steadily. "I did. You looked happy. At home. I couldn't resist capturing that moment."

His expression softened, a mix of surprise and something deeper, more tender. "You really do have a gift, Rakel. For seeing the beauty in things others might miss."

We began the walk back to the main part of the orchard, our steps slow and meandering, as if neither of us wanted the afternoon to end. As we walked, Tevin pointed out more features of the land of a gnarled old tree that produced the sweetest apples, a hidden stream that ran through the property, the distant silhouette of the barn he wanted to renovate.

"I've been thinking about your idea for the wood transfers," he said as we neared the farmhouse. "I think they'd be perfect for decorating the barn once we fix it up. Maybe we could even do a whole series of them, showing the orchard through the seasons."

A thrill of excitement at the idea put a smile on my face. "That would be amazing, Tevin. I'd love to collaborate on something like that."

He grinned, his enthusiasm infectious. "I was hoping you'd say that. Maybe we could start planning it out at the festival next weekend? Over some cider and caramel apples?"

"It's a date," I said, then immediately felt my face flush. "I mean, not a date date, but you know what I mean."

Tevin chuckled, his eyes twinkling with amusement. "I know what you mean, Rakel. And I'm looking forward to it, whatever we want to call it."

As we reached my car, I felt a pang of reluctance to leave. The afternoon had been magical in more ways than one, and I wasn't quite ready for it to end.

"Thank you again for the tour," I said, fiddling with my car keys. "It was really inspiring. I can't wait to go through all these photos and start planning some shoots here."

Tevin nodded, his expression warm. "I'm glad you enjoyed it. And I meant what I said earlier, you're welcome here anytime. For photoshoots or just because."

Our eyes met, and for a moment, the air between us seemed charged with possibility. I wondered what would happen if I took a step closer, if I let myself act on the attraction I'd been feeling all afternoon.

But before I could do anything, the sound of a truck broke the moment pulling up nearby. An older man climbed out, waving to Tevin.

"Hey there, Tev! Got those new seedlings you ordered," the man called out.

Tevin sighed, looking apologetic. "Duty calls, I'm afraid. But I'll see you at the festival next weekend?"

I nodded, trying not to let my disappointment show. "Definitely. I'm really looking forward to it."

As I climbed into my car and started the engine, I watched in the rearview mirror as Tevin greeted the delivery man. Just before I pulled away, he turned and caught my eye, raising a hand in farewell. I waved back, my heart fluttering in my chest.

Driving back into town, my mind raced with thoughts and emotions. The orchard had been even more beautiful than I'd imagined, full of potential for amazing photographs. But more than that, I couldn't stop thinking about Tevin and his passion for the land, his kind eyes, the way he'd made me feel seen and appreciated.

I tried to remind myself that we were just friends, that he'd invited me to the festival as a friendly gesture. But a small voice in the back of my mind whispered that maybe, just maybe, there could be something more brewing between us.

As I pulled up to my apartment above the studio, I realized I was smiling. For the first time in a long while, I felt truly excited about the future - both professionally and personally. The fall festival was just a week away, and I couldn't wait to see what it might bring.

Climbing the stairs to my apartment, I paused at the window, looking out at the town of Maple Grove spread out before me. The setting sun painted the sky in shades of pink and gold, reminding me of the breathtaking view from Tevin's hilltop. At that moment, I felt a sense of belonging I hadn't experienced since moving here.

CHAPTER FOUR

*T*evin
　　　I smiled as I watched Rakel's eyes light up at the sight of the Maple Grove Fall Festival. Twinkling lights strung between lamp posts and the scent of cinnamon and apples wafting through the crisp October air transformed the town square. It was like seeing the festival for the first time again through her eyes, and I found myself more excited than I'd been in years.

"Oh, Tevin, this is amazing!" Rakel exclaimed, her camera already in hand. She snapped a quick photo of the entrance, where a large banner welcomed visitors to the festival. "I can't believe I missed this last year."

I chuckled, feeling a warmth in my chest that had nothing to do with the steaming cup of cider in my hand. "Well, I'm glad I could introduce you to it properly this year. Come on, let me show you the best parts."

As we made our way through the crowd, I couldn't help but notice the way Rakel's curly auburn hair caught the light, or how her hazel eyes sparkled with excitement. I'd been looking forward to this evening all week, and now that it was here, it felt even better than I'd imagined.

We stopped at a booth where old Mrs. Guthrie was selling her famous apple pies. "Tevin Short, as I live and breathe!" she called out, her wrinkled face breaking into a wide grin. "And who's this lovely young lady?"

A blush crept up my neck as I introduced Rakel. Mrs. Guthrie's eyes twinkled knowingly, and I knew the town gossip mill would work overtime tonight. But as Rakel chatted animatedly with Mrs. Guthrie about her pies and the history of the festival, I found I didn't mind one bit.

As we continued our tour of the festival, I pointed out the various attractions. "Over there's the pumpkin carving contest," I said, gesturing to a group of tables where people hunched over, intently working on their creations. "And later tonight, there'll be a bonfire and hayrides."

Rakel nodded, snapping photos as we walked. "This is perfect, Tevin. I can already imagine a whole series of shots capturing the spirit of the festival."

We stopped at a few more booths, sampling local treats and chatting with townspeople. I couldn't help but notice how easily Rakel fit in, her warm smile and genuine interest in people's stories, winning them over quickly. It made something in my chest tighten, a feeling I wasn't quite ready to name yet.

As the sky darkened and the festival lights grew brighter, we found ourselves at the edge of the dance floor. A local band was playing a mix of country and folk tunes, and couples were twirling around, laughing, and having a good time.

I turned to Rakel, suddenly feeling nervous. "So, uh, would you like to dance?"

She looked surprised for a moment, then smiled. "I'd love to, but I have to warn you, I'm not very good."

I grinned, feeling relief wash over me. "That's okay, neither am I. We can be bad together."

As I took her hand and led her onto the dance floor, a jolt of energy flashed through me. We started moving to the music, awkward at first, but soon finding our rhythm. Rakel laughed as I attempted to twirl her, and the sound made my heart soar.

"You know," I said as we swayed to a slower song, "I'm really glad you came tonight, Rakel. It's been a long time since I've enjoyed the festival this much."

She looked up at me, her eyes soft in the twinkling lights. "I'm glad too, Tevin. Thank you for showing me around. It's been wonderful."

For a moment, the rest of the festival faded away, and it was just the two of us, moving together to the music. I leaned in slightly, drawn by the warmth in her eyes and the soft curve of her smile.

But before I could do anything, a voice cut through the moment like a knife. "Rakel? Is that you?"

We both turned, and I felt Rakel stiffen in my arms. A man was making his way through the crowd towards us, his eyes fixed on Rakel. He was tall and well-dressed, with the good looks that probably opened a lot of doors for him.

"Jake?" Rakel's voice was barely above a whisper, her face pale in the festival lights. "What are you doing here?"

Jake reached us, his smile not quite reaching his eyes. "I've been trying to get in touch with you for weeks. When I heard you'd moved here, I thought I'd come see for myself." His gaze flicked to me, then back to Rakel. "Aren't you going to introduce us?"

I felt a surge of protectiveness as Rakel seemed to shrink into herself. "I'm Tevin Short," I said, extending my hand. "I own the apple orchard just outside of town."

Jake shook my hand, his grip a little too firm. "Jake Holloway. I'm Rakel's... well, we have a history."

I didn't miss the way Rakel flinched at his words, or the look of discomfort on her face. "It's nice to meet you," I said, even though it wasn't nice at all. "Rakel and I were just enjoying the festival. There's a lot to see."

Jake's smile turned bitter. "Oh, I'm sure. But I was hoping to catch up with Rakel. For old times' sake."

Rakel's hand tightened on my arm. "Jake, I don't think that's a good idea," she said, her voice stronger now. "I'm here with Tevin."

Jake's eyes narrowed slightly, and I felt a surge of satisfaction. But it was short-lived as he turned his charm back on. "Come on, Rak. Just a few minutes? For all we've been through?"

I could feel the tension radiating off Rakel, and I wanted nothing more than to whisk her away from this guy. But I knew it wasn't my place to make that decision for her.

"It's okay," I said softly, even though it felt anything but okay. "If you want to talk to him, I can wait for you by the cider stand."

Rakel looked up at me, conflict clear in her eyes. "Are you sure? I don't want to leave you alone."

I forced a smile. "I'll be fine. Take your time."

As Rakel reluctantly walked away with Jake, I felt a knot form in the pit of my stomach. I made my way to the cider stand, trying to push down the feelings of jealousy and worry that were bubbling up inside me.

I ordered a cup of cider, more for something to do with my hands than because I wanted it. As I stood there, sipping the too-sweet drink, I couldn't help but scan the crowd for Rakel and Jake.

I spotted them near the edge of the festival grounds,

partially hidden by a large oak tree. Jake was talking animatedly, his hands moving as he spoke. Rakel stood with her arms crossed, her body language closed off.

I knew I shouldn't eavesdrop. It was wrong, and Rakel deserved her privacy. But as I saw Jake step closer to her, placing a hand on her arm, I moved before I could think better of it.

I didn't get too close, but I positioned myself where I could hear their conversation, pretending to be interested in a nearby craft booth.

"...can't believe you just ran away like that," Jake was saying, his voice low and intense. "We had something special, Rakel. You can't just throw it away."

"I didn't throw anything away, Jake," Rakel replied, her voice tired. "We wanted different things. It wasn't working."

Jake scoffed. "And this is better? Living in some small town, taking pictures of apples? Come on, Rak. You're better than this."

I felt my fists clench at my sides. Who did this guy think he was?

"I like it here," Rakel said, and I could hear the steel in her voice. "I'm happy here. My work is going well, and I've made friends."

"Friends like that farmer?" Jake's voice dripped with disdain. "Is that really what you want? To settle for some country bumpkin when you could have so much more?"

I felt like she punched me in the gut. Is that how Rakel saw me? Some country bumpkin she was settling for?

But Rakel's next words made my heart soar. "Tevin is kind, and genuine, and he believes in me. That's worth more than all the fancy parties and connections you're offering."

Jake was quiet for a moment, and when he spoke again,

his voice was softer, almost pleading. "I miss you, Rakel. I know I messed up, but I've changed. Give me another chance. Come back to the city with me. We can start over."

I held my breath, waiting for Rakel's response. Part of me wanted to step in, to tell Jake to back off. But I knew this was Rakel's decision to make.

"Jake, I..." Rakel's voice trailed off, and I felt my heart clench.

I couldn't bear to hear anymore. I turned and walked away, my mind racing. What if Rakel decided to go back with him? What if she realized that life in Maple Grove, that I, wasn't enough for her?

As I made my way back to the center of the festival, I tried to push those thoughts aside. Rakel was her own person, and whatever she decided, I would respect it. But the thought of her leaving, of losing whatever was growing between us, felt like a physical ache in my chest.

I warmed my hands by the bonfire, watching the flames dance and trying to sort out my jumbled emotions. I was so lost in thought that I didn't notice someone approaching until I felt a hand on my arm.

"Tevin?"

I turned to find Rakel standing there, her eyes searching my face. "Hey," I said, trying to keep my voice neutral. "Everything okay?"

She nodded, then shook her head, then laughed a little. "Not really. But it will be." She took a deep breath. "I'm sorry about that. I had no idea Jake would show up here."

I shrugged, trying to appear nonchalant. "It's okay. You two obviously have history. It's natural that you'd want to talk."

Rakel's brow furrowed. "Tevin, I hope you know that Jake showing up doesn't change anything. I meant what I said about being happy here."

My heart leapt at her words, but I tried to keep my face calm. "You don't owe me any explanations, Rakel. We're friends, and I just want you to be happy."

She stepped closer, her eyes never leaving mine. "What if I want to be more than friends?"

For a moment, I couldn't breathe. "What about Jake?" I asked.

Rakel shook her head. "Jake is my past. I told him that. I'm more interested in my future, and I hope you might be part of it."

Before I could overthink it, I reached out and pulled her close. Her lips met mine, soft and sweet, and my heart thumped. The sounds of the festival faded away, and all I could focus on was the feel of Rakel in my arms, the scent of her hair, the warmth of her body against mine.

When we finally pulled apart, we were both a little breathless. Rakel smiled up at me, her eyes shining in the firelight. "So," she said, a teasing note in her voice, "does this mean you'll let me take pictures of you in that lucky flannel shirt of yours?"

I laughed, feeling lighter than I had in years. "For you? Anything."

As we turned to rejoin the festival, hand in hand, I couldn't help but feel that something had shifted. The future stretched out before us, full of possibility and promise. And for the first time in a long time, I was excited to see where it might lead.

But as we walked away from the bonfire, I caught sight of Jake watching us from the shadows. His expression was dark, and I felt a chill run down my spine. Something told me this wasn't the last we'd see of him, and I tightened my grip on Rakel's hand, silently vowing to protect her from whatever might come our way.

For now, though, I pushed those thoughts aside.

Tonight was about celebrating, about new beginnings. Rakel leaned her head on my shoulder, pointing out a beautiful display of carved pumpkins.

The festival continued around us, a whirl of lights and laughter and music. But for me, the real magic was right here, in the warmth of Rakel's hand in mine and the promise of tomorrow in her smile. As we made our way through the crowd, I couldn't help but think that maybe, just maybe, this was the start of something truly special.

CHAPTER FIVE

*R*akel

I clutched the steering wheel of my beat-up Subaru, my heart racing as I pulled into the familiar gravel driveway of Tevin's orchard. The crisp October air nipped at my cheeks as I stepped out of the car, the scent of ripe apples and autumn leaves filling my senses. I took a deep breath, trying to calm my nerves.

This wasn't just another photo shoot. This was a date. A real, honest-to-goodness date with Tevin Short.

I spotted him waiting by the old red barn, looking absolutely irresistible in his worn jeans and that lucky flannel shirt he'd mentioned. When he saw me, his face broke into a wide grin that made my stomach do a little flip.

"Rakel!" he called out, jogging over to meet me. "I was starting to think you might have gotten lost."

I laughed, feeling some of my nervousness melt away. "In a town this small? Not likely. Though I did have to take a detour around Old Man Johnson's tractor. Again."

Tevin chuckled, shaking his head. "That thing's been

breaking down in the middle of the road since I was a kid. Some things never change."

As he spoke, his eyes crinkled at the corners when he smiled, and the morning sunlight caught the golden flecks in his warm brown eyes. A blush warmed my cheeks, and I glanced away, pretending to fiddle with my camera bag.

"So," I said, trying to sound casual, "what's on the agenda for today? Besides picking apples, of course."

Tevin's eyes twinkled with mischief. "Oh, I've got a few surprises up my sleeve. But first things first, we need to get you properly outfitted for apple picking."

He reached behind him and produced a worn straw hat, placing it gently on my head. The brim flopped down, nearly covering my eyes, and I couldn't help but giggle.

"How do I look?" I asked, striking a pose.

Tevin's gaze softened, and he reached out to tuck a stray curl behind my ear. "Beautiful," he said softly, and I felt my heart skip a beat.

Clearing his throat, he gestured towards the orchard. "Shall we?"

As we made our way through the rows of trees, Tevin pointed out different varieties of apples, explaining their unique characteristics and best uses. He captivated not just by the information, but by the passion in his voice as he spoke about his family's legacy.

"And these," he said, stopping in front of a row of trees with deep red apples, "are my personal favorites. Crimson Crisps. They're perfect for eating fresh, but they also make a mean apple pie."

I reached up, plucking one from a low-hanging branch. "May I?"

Tevin nodded, watching intently as I took a bite. The apple was indeed crisp, with a perfect balance of sweet and tart that exploded across my taste buds.

"Oh my gosh," I mumbled around the mouthful of apple, "that's incredible."

Tevin's face lit up with pride. "I knew you'd like them. Here, let me show you the best way to pick them."

He stepped closer, reaching up to show the proper twisting motion to remove an apple from its stem. I tried to focus on his instructions, but his proximity distracted me with the warmth radiating from his body, the earthy scent of his cologne mingling with the crisp autumn air.

As I reached up to try picking an apple myself, my hand brushed against his, sending a jolt of electricity through me. Our eyes met, and for a moment, the world seemed to stand still.

Then a mischievous glint appeared in Tevin's eyes. Before I could react, he plucked the apple from my hand and took a big bite, juice dribbling down his chin.

"Hey!" I protested, laughing. "That was mine!"

Tevin grinned, holding the apple just out of my reach. "You'll have to be quicker than that, city girl."

I lunged for the apple, but Tevin danced away, laughing. What ensued was a playful chase through the orchard, our laughter echoing through the trees as we darted between rows, ducking under branches and trying to outmaneuver each other.

Finally, I cornered him against the trunk of a large apple tree. "Gotcha!" I declared triumphantly, snatching the apple from his hand.

We were both breathless from running and laughing, our faces flushed with exertion and something more. As our laughter subsided, I realized how close we were standing, my hand still resting on his chest where I'd grabbed the apple.

Tevin's eyes locked onto mine, his expression softening.

"You know," he said softly, "I'm really glad you came today, Rakel."

I swallowed hard, my heart pounding. "Me too," I whispered.

The moment stretched between us, charged with possibility. Then, a loud squawk from a nearby bird broke the spell, making us both jump.

Tevin cleared his throat, taking a step back. "We should, uh, probably get back to picking apples. I've got a special treat planned for later."

I nodded, trying to ignore the pang of disappointment at the interrupted moment. "Lead the way, apple master."

We spent the next hour picking apples, filling our baskets with a variety of types for different uses, with some for baking, some for cider, and plenty for eating fresh. As we worked, we fell into simple conversation, sharing stories from our childhoods and our dreams for the future.

I told Tevin about my first camera, a beat-up Polaroid I'd found at a garage sale when I was ten, and how I'd spent an entire summer taking blurry pictures of everything in sight. He regaled me with tales of mischief he and his sister Liv had gotten into as kids, like the time they'd tried to turn the old barn into a *haunted house* for Halloween and ended up scaring themselves more than anyone else.

As the sun climbed higher in the sky, Tevin suggested we take a break. He led me to a small clearing where he'd set up a picnic blanket under the shade of a gnarled old apple tree.

"Wait here," he said with a wink, disappearing back towards the barn.

I snapped a few photos of the orchard, capturing the way the sunlight filtered through the leaves and the vibrant colors of the apples against the clear blue sky. When I turned back, Tevin was approaching with a thermos and two mugs.

"I hope you're thirsty," he said, settling down on the blanket beside me. "It's time for that special treat I mentioned."

He poured a steaming amber liquid into the mugs, and the rich aroma of apples and spices filled the air. I took a cautious sip and felt warmth spread through my body.

"Oh wow," I said, taking another, longer sip. "This is amazing. What is it?"

Tevin beamed with pride. "My own special recipe for hot spiced cider. I've been experimenting with unique blends of apples and spices. What do you think?"

I closed my eyes, savoring the complex flavors. "I think you've got a gold mine on your hands. This is seriously the best cider I've ever tasted."

His eyes lit up at the compliment. "You really think so? I've been toying with the idea of bottling it, maybe selling it at farmer's markets or local shops. But I wasn't sure if people would be interested."

"Are you kidding?" I said, taking another sip. "People would go crazy for this. You could build a whole brand around it."

Tevin's expression turned thoughtful. "You know, that's not a bad idea. I've been looking for ways to diversify the orchard's income, especially during the off-season."

As he spoke, I found myself captivated by his passion and vision for the future of his family's business. He respected the traditions that had been passed down through generations, but he also wasn't afraid to innovate and try new things.

We continued to chat as we sipped our cider. The conversation flowed easily between us. I opened up to Tevin in a way I hadn't with anyone in a long time, sharing my hopes and fears about my photography business and my life in Maple Grove.

"Sometimes I wonder if I made the right choice," I admitted, tracing the rim of my mug with my finger. "Moving to a small town, starting over. It's been harder than I expected."

Tevin's hand covered mine, his touch warm and reassuring. "For what it's worth," he said softly, "I think you're incredibly brave. It takes a lot of courage to chase your dreams, especially when it means leaving everything familiar behind."

I looked up, meeting his gaze. The sincerity in his eyes made my breath catch in my throat. "Thank you," I whispered. "That means a lot, coming from you."

We fell silent for a moment, the air between us charged with unspoken emotions. Tevin's thumb traced small circles on the back of my hand, sending shivers up my arm.

Slowly, almost imperceptibly, we leaned towards each other. My heart raced as Tevin's free hand came up to cup my cheek, his touch feather-light. Our eyes met, and I saw my desire reflected in his warm brown gaze.

"Rakel," he murmured, his voice husky. "I've been wanting to do this since the moment I met you."

And then his lips were on mine, soft and sweet and tasting faintly of apples and cinnamon. The world seemed to fade away as I melted into the kiss, my hands coming up to tangle in his hair.

The kiss deepened, and I felt a warmth spreading through my body that had nothing to do with the cider. Tevin's arms wrapped around me, pulling me closer, and I sighed contentedly against his lips.

When we finally broke apart, we were both breathless. Tevin rested his forehead against mine, a soft smile playing on his lips.

"Wow," I whispered, feeling a bit dazed.

Tevin chuckled, the sound sending a pleasant vibration through me. "Yeah," he agreed. "Wow indeed."

We stayed like that for a moment, savoring the closeness. Then Tevin pulled back slightly, his expression turning serious.

"Rakel," he said, taking my hands in his. "There's something I want to talk to you about."

I felt a flutter of nervousness in my stomach. "Oh? What is it?"

Tevin took a deep breath, as if steeling himself. "I've been thinking a lot about what you said earlier, about my cider and building a brand. And, well, I have a proposition for you."

My eyebrows shot up in surprise. "A proposition?"

He nodded, his eyes bright with excitement. "I want to start a line of artisanal ciders and other apple-based products. But to do it right, I need help with branding, marketing, and creating a cohesive visual identity. And I can't think of anyone better suited for that than you."

I blinked, trying to process what he was saying. "Me? But I'm a photographer, not a marketing expert."

Tevin squeezed my hands. "You're not just a photographer, Rakel. You're an artist with an incredible eye for composition and detail. You understand how to capture the essence of a moment, of a place. That's exactly what I need for this project."

My mind raced with possibilities. Images of rustic bottles with beautifully designed labels, lifestyle photos showcasing the cider in cozy autumn settings, a cohesive Instagram feed that told the story of the orchard and its products. It all came flooding into my imagination.

"I don't know what to say," I stammered, feeling both excited and overwhelmed.

Tevin's expression softened. "You don't have to decide right now. I know it's a big ask, and I understand if you need time to think about it. But I really believe we could create something special together, Rakel. Not just personally, but professionally too."

I nodded slowly, my thoughts swirling. It was a tempting offer, one that might solve a lot of my financial worries and give my career a much-needed boost. But it also came with its own set of complications. Working with Tevin would mean blurring the lines between our personal and professional lives, something I'd sworn I'd never do again after my disastrous relationship with Jake.

But as I looked into Tevin's earnest face, I felt a spark of hope ignite in my chest. This differed from what I'd had with Jake. Tevin respected my work, valued my input. He saw me as a partner, not just a pretty face to hang on his arm at gallery openings.

"Can I have some time to think about it?" I asked finally.

Tevin nodded, relief clear in his expression. "Of course. Take all the time you need. There's no pressure, I promise."

He leaned in and kissed me softly, a brief, sweet gesture that left me wanting more. As he pulled away, a mischievous glint appeared in his eyes.

"In the meantime," he said, climbing to his feet and offering me his hand, "what do you say we finish picking those apples? I bet I can fill my basket faster than you can."

I grinned, accepting his hand and letting him pull me up. "Oh, you're on, Short. Prepare to eat my dust!"

As we raced back towards the apple trees, laughing and teasing each other, I felt a lightness in my chest that I hadn't experienced in years.

CHAPTER SIX

*T*evin

I stood in the middle of Rakel's studio, surrounded by a sea of photographs spread out on every available surface. My eyes darted from image to image, each one capturing a different aspect of the orchard in stunning detail. There was something surreal about seeing my family's legacy through Rakel's lens, familiar scenes transformed into works of art.

"What do you think?" Rakel asked, biting her lower lip as she watched me take it all in. "I know it's a lot, but I wanted to show you the range of possibilities we have to work with."

I picked up a close-up shot of an apple, the morning dew still clinging to its skin. "Rakel, these are incredible. I mean, I knew you were talented, but this..." I shook my head, at a loss for words.

She beamed at me, her hazel eyes sparkling with excitement. "I'm so glad you like them. I was thinking we could use different series for different products. Like, these more artistic shots for the premium cider line, and maybe some of the lifestyle images for the regular products."

As she spoke, gesturing animatedly to different photos, a warmth spread through my chest. Seeing her so passionate about our project, about my family's orchard, it was almost overwhelming.

"You've really put a lot of thought into this," I said, unable to keep the awe out of my voice.

Rakel nodded, tucking a stray curl behind her ear. "Well, ever since you proposed this collaboration, I haven't been able to stop thinking about it. The possibilities are endless, Tevin. We could really create something special here."

I moved closer to her, drawn in by her enthusiasm. "I couldn't agree more. And seeing all of this..." I gestured to the photos surrounding us, "it's making it feel real in a way it hasn't before."

She looked up at me, her expression softening. "Are you okay with that? I know this is a big step for the orchard, for your family's business."

I took a deep breath, considering her question. "I am. It's exciting and a little terrifying, but I really believe in this. In us," I added, reaching out to take her hand.

Rakel squeezed my hand, a small smile playing on her lips. "I'm glad. Because I have about a million more ideas I want to run by you."

We spent the next hour poring over the photos, discussing different concepts for labels, packaging, and marketing materials. Rakel's creativity seemed boundless, and I got caught up in her vision.

As we were debating the merits of a more rustic versus modern aesthetic for the premium cider line, my phone buzzed in my pocket. I pulled it out, glancing at the screen, and felt my stomach drop.

"Everything okay?" Rakel asked, noticing my change in demeanor.

I sighed, shoving the phone back in my pocket without answering. "It's my sister, Liv. She's been trying to reach me all day."

Rakel's brow furrowed with concern. "Is something wrong?"

I ran a hand through my hair, feeling the familiar tension creep into my shoulders. "Not exactly. It's just complicated."

Rakel stood up from where she'd been crouching over a layout of photos, moving to stand in front of me. "Do you want to talk about it?"

I hesitated, years of keeping family matters private warring with my growing desire to open up to Rakel. Finally, I nodded, sinking down onto the worn leather couch in the corner of her studio.

"Liv and I, we've always been close," I began, staring down at my hands. "But lately, things have been strained. Ever since I started talking about making changes at the orchard, trying new things."

Rakel sat down beside me, her presence a comforting warmth. "She doesn't approve of the cider line?"

I shook my head, letting out a humorless chuckle. "It's not just that. It's everything. The event space in the barn, the new varieties of apples I want to try, even..." I trailed off, glancing at her.

"Even me?" Rakel asked softly.

I nodded, feeling a pang of guilt. "She thinks I'm being impulsive, throwing away years of tradition for... how did she put it? *Some flight of fancy and a pretty face.*"

Rakel winced, but didn't look surprised. "That must be hard, not having her support."

"It is," I admitted, feeling a weight lift as I finally voiced my frustrations. "Liv's always been the practical one, the one who had everything figured out. And me? I was just the dreamer, the one with his head in the clouds."

I stood up, too restless to sit still, and began pacing the small space. "You know, when our parents died, Liv was the one who stepped up. She was only twenty-two, but she took charge of everything with the orchard, the finances, even taking care of me. I was nineteen and a mess, and she held it all together."

Rakel watched me, her eyes full of understanding. "That's a lot of responsibility for someone so young."

I nodded, feeling a lump form in my throat. "It was. And I'll always be grateful for what she did. But now..." I trailed off, struggling to find the right words.

"Now you're grown up, and you want to make your own decisions," Rakel finished for me.

"Exactly," I said, relieved that she understood. "But Liv, she still sees me as that nineteen-year-old kid who needed taking care of. She can't accept that I might actually know what I'm doing, that I might have good ideas for the orchard."

Rakel stood up, crossing the room to stand in front of me. She reached out, taking both of my hands in hers. "Tevin, from everything you've told me about the orchard, about your plans for it, it's clear that you love it just as much as Liv does. You're not trying to throw away tradition; you're trying to honor it while also moving forward."

My eyes stung with unexpected tears. "I just wish she could see that. I wish she could understand that I'm not trying to destroy everything our family has built. I'm trying to ensure it survives for another generation."

Rakel pulled me into a hug, and I let myself sink into her embrace, drawing comfort from her warmth. We stood like that for a long moment, the tension slowly draining from my body.

When we finally pulled apart, Rakel's eyes were bright with an idea. "Tevin, what if we included Liv in this project?"

I blinked, surprised by the suggestion. "What do you mean?"

Rakel's excitement grew as she spoke. "Well, you said Liv is the practical one, right? The one who's good with finances and management? What if we brought her in as a partner? She could handle the business side of things while we focus on the creative aspects."

I considered her words, turning the idea over in my mind. "I don't know, Rakel. Liv's pretty set in her ways. I'm not sure she'd be open to it."

"But that's just it," Rakel pressed on. "By including her, we're showing that we value her expertise, that this isn't about pushing her out or ignoring tradition. It's about combining the best of both worlds – her business acumen with our new ideas."

The more I thought about it, the more sense it made. "It could work," I said slowly. "If we could get Liv on board, it would solve a lot of our problems. She'd be involved from the ground up, able to see firsthand that we're not just acting on impulse."

Rakel nodded eagerly. "Exactly. And who knows? Maybe once she sees the potential in this project, she'll be more open to some of your other ideas for the orchard."

I felt a spark of hope ignite in my chest. "It's worth a shot," I said, a smile tugging at the corners of my mouth. "Honestly, how do you always know exactly what to say?"

She grinned, a faint blush coloring her cheeks. "I guess you just bring out the best in me, Tevin Short."

I pulled her close, pressing a soft kiss to her forehead.

"Thank you," I murmured against her skin. "For listening, for understanding. For everything."

Rakel tilted her head up, capturing my lips in a tender kiss. When we parted, she smiled up at me. "That's what partners are for, right?"

The word *partners* sent a thrill through me. It encompassed so much in our budding romance, our professional collaboration, the way we seemed to balance each other out perfectly.

"Right," I agreed, feeling lighter than I had in weeks. "Partners."

As if on cue, my phone buzzed again. This time, instead of ignoring it, I pulled it out and looked at the screen. Liv's name flashed up at me, a reminder of the conversation we needed to have.

"I should probably call her back," I said, glancing at Rakel.

She nodded, giving my hand a supportive squeeze. "Do you want me to give you some privacy?"

I shook my head. "No, stay. Please. I think I'd like you here for this."

Rakel smiled, leading me back to the couch. We sat down together, and I took a deep breath before hitting the call button.

Liv answered on the second ring. "Tevin? Finally, I've been trying to reach you all day."

"I know, I'm sorry," I said, trying to keep my voice calm. "I've been in meetings about the new cider line."

There was a pause on the other end of the line, and I could almost see Liv's disapproving frown. "Right. The cider line. That's actually what I wanted to talk to you about."

I braced myself for an argument, but Rakel's hand on my arm steadied me. "Okay," I said. "I'm listening."

"I've been thinking," Liv began, her voice hesitant. "Maybe I was too quick to dismiss your idea. I still have concerns, but I'm willing to hear you out. Properly this time."

I felt my jaw drop, stunned by this unexpected olive branch. "Really? Liv, that's... thank you. That means a lot."

"Don't thank me yet," she warned, but I could hear a hint of amusement in her voice. "I still think you're being impulsive, but... you're not a kid anymore, Tev. I need to start trusting your judgment."

I swallowed hard, emotion welling up in my throat. "I appreciate that, Liv. And actually, I have an idea I'd like to run by you. About the cider line, and your role in it."

There was a pause, and then Liv asked, curiosity clear in her tone, "Oh? What kind of idea?"

I looked at Rakel, who nodded encouragingly. Taking a deep breath, I launched into an explanation of our plan to bring Liv on as a partner in the venture.

As I spoke, I could almost feel the shift in Liv's attitude through the phone. By the time I finished outlining the proposal, there was a new energy in her voice.

"You know," she said slowly, "that actually sounds... promising. I'd need to see the numbers, of course, and we'd have to hash out the details, but I like the idea of being involved from the start."

I felt a grin spread across my face. "Really? That's great, Liv. I was hoping you'd say that."

"Don't get too excited yet, little brother," she warned, but I could hear the smile in her voice. "We've still got a lot to discuss. But I'm willing to give it a shot if you are."

"Absolutely," I said, feeling a weight lift off my shoulders. "How about we set up a meeting next week? You can come to the orchard, meet Rakel, and we can go over everything in detail."

"Sounds good," Liv agreed. "And Tevin? I'm proud of you. For taking initiative, for not giving up on your ideas even when I was being stubborn. Mom and Dad would be proud too."

My eyes stung with tears. "Thanks, Liv. That means everything to me."

After we said our goodbyes and hung up, I turned to Rakel, who was watching me with a mix of anticipation and concern.

"Well?" she asked. "How did it go?"

I let out a laugh, feeling almost giddy with relief. "It went amazingly. She's open to the idea, Rakel. She wants to meet next week to discuss details."

Rakel's face lit up, and she threw her arms around me. "Tevin, that's wonderful! I'm so happy for you."

I hugged her back tightly, marveling at how much had changed in just a few short hours. "I couldn't have done it without you," I murmured into her hair. "Your idea to include Liv, your support has made all the difference."

Rakel pulled back slightly, her eyes shining. "We're partners, remember? Your victories are my victories."

I nodded, feeling a surge of emotion. "Partners," I agreed, leaning in to kiss her softly.

As our lips met, and a sense of rightness settled over me. Here, in this moment, with Rakel in my arms and the promise of reconciliation with Liv on the horizon, I knew we were on the cusp of something truly special.

But as we broke apart, a nagging thought crept into my mind. Things were falling into place almost too perfectly. What if it was all too good to be true? What if involving Liv in the business caused more problems than it solved? And what about Jake, Rakel's ex? He had seemed awfully interested in her at the fall festival. Could he still pose a threat to our budding relationship?

I pushed those thoughts aside, determined to focus on the positive. We had overcome one hurdle, but I knew there would be more challenges ahead. For now, though, I was content to bask in this moment of hope and possibility, with Rakel by my side and a future full of promise stretching out before us.

CHAPTER SEVEN

*R*akel
    I smoothed down my dress for the hundredth time, my heart racing as I peeked out the window of the newly renovated barn. A steady stream of cars was pulling into the makeshift parking area we'd set up in the orchard, and I could see people making their way towards us, bundled up against the crisp November evening.

"Deep breaths, Rakel," I muttered to myself, trying to calm my nerves. This was it. The grand opening of our joint venture with Tevin's artisanal cider line and my photography studio, all housed in this beautifully restored barn on the Short family orchard.

"Hey," Tevin's voice came from behind me, warm and reassuring. I turned to see him approaching, looking devastatingly handsome in a tailored suit that complemented his rugged charm. "You ready for this?"

I nodded, managing a wobbly smile. "As ready as I'll ever be. You?"

He grinned, reaching out to take my hand. "With you by my side? I'm ready for anything."

His confidence was contagious, and I felt some of my anxiety melt away as he squeezed my hand. We'd worked so hard for this moment, pouring our hearts and souls into every detail. From the rustic-chic decor that seamlessly blended the barn's history with modern touches to the carefully curated selection of ciders and my latest photography collection, all represented the perfect fusion of our passions and talents.

"Looks like we've got quite the turnout," Tevin said, glancing out the window. "Half of Maple Grove must be here."

I followed his gaze, my breath catching as I saw the growing crowd. Friends, family, and community members were all gathered, their excited chatter drifting up to us even through the closed windows.

"Is that your sister?" I asked, spotting a tall woman with Tevin's warm brown eyes making her way through the crowd.

Tevin nodded, a mix of emotions playing across his face. "Yep, that's Liv. I'm glad she came. I wasn't sure she would, even after everything."

I squeezed his hand, remembering the rocky path we'd traveled to get Liv on board with our venture. It had taken weeks of meetings, spreadsheets, and late-night discussions, but in the end, we'd found a balance that worked for all of us. Liv's business acumen had proven invaluable in turning our creative vision into a viable business plan.

"She wouldn't miss this for the world," I assured him. "She's proud of you, Tevin. Of us."

He smiled down at me, his eyes crinkling at the corners in that way that never failed to make my heart skip a beat.

"Speaking of proud," he said, "have I told you how amazing you look tonight?"

A blush crept up my cheeks. I'd splurged on a new dress for the occasion in a deep burgundy number that hugged my curves and made me feel like a million bucks. "You clean up pretty well yourself, farm boy," I teased, reaching up to straighten his tie.

A knock at the door interrupted the moment. "You two decent in there?" came the playful voice of Tevin's best friend, Sam. "Because we've got a whole crowd of people out here waiting to see what all the fuss is about."

Tevin chuckled, calling back, "We'll be right out!"

He turned to me, his expression growing serious. "You ready to do this thing, partner?"

I took a deep breath, squaring my shoulders. "Let's knock their socks off."

Hand in hand, we walked to the barn doors. With one last shared glance, we pushed them open, stepping out onto the small stage we'd set up for the occasion.

A cheer went up from the crowd as we appeared, and I felt a surge of warmth at the sight of so many familiar faces. There was Mrs. Johnson from the library, who'd been one of my first photography clients in Maple Grove. Next to her stood Old Man Peters, who, despite his grumpy exterior, had become one of our most enthusiastic taste-testers for Tevin's experimental cider flavors.

I spotted my parents in the crowd, my mom dabbing at her eyes with a tissue while my dad beamed with pride. They'd been skeptical when I'd first moved to Maple Grove to pursue my photography dreams, but seeing them here tonight, supporting this new chapter of my life, meant everything.

Tevin cleared his throat, stepping forward to address the crowd. "Good evening, everyone," he began, his voice strong and clear. "Rakel and I want to thank you all for coming out tonight to celebrate the grand opening of Short & Sweet Ciders and Rakel Boswell Photography."

Another cheer went up, and a swell of pride warmed my heart. This was really happening.

"When I first took over the orchard from my parents," Tevin continued, "I knew I wanted to honor their legacy while also bringing something new to the table. I just never imagined I'd find the perfect partner to help make that dream a reality."

He turned to me, his eyes shining with affection. "Rakel, your creativity, your vision, and your unwavering support have made all of this possible. I couldn't ask for a better partner in business or in life."

Tears pricked at my eyes, overwhelmed by the sincerity in his voice. Tevin gave my hand another squeeze before turning back to the crowd.

"But enough sappy stuff," he said with a grin, earning a laugh from the audience. "You're all here to see what we've been working on, right? Well, without further ado, let's get this party started!"

With that, we descended from the stage, and the barn doors swung fully open, revealing the transformed interior. Gasps and murmurs of appreciation rippled through the crowd as people filed in.

Two main areas divided the barn. On one side, Tevin set up his cider tasting station, with rows of gleaming bottles and a beautiful bar made from reclaimed wood from the old apple press. On the other side, my photography studio and gallery space showcased my latest collection of autumn-themed images.

As people spread out, exploring the space, I found myself drawn to my gallery area. Large prints of my favorite shots from the past few months with the misty mornings in the orchard, close-ups of dew-covered apples, and candid moments of life in Maple Grove adorned the walls.

"These are absolutely stunning, Rakel," a voice said beside me. I turned to see Liv, Tevin's sister, studying one of my photos intently.

"Thank you," I said, feeling a mix of pride and nervousness. Despite our improved relationship, I still felt a need to prove myself to Tevin's strong-willed sister.

Liv turned to me, her expression softening. "I mean it. You have a real talent for capturing the essence of this place. I can see why Tevin was so insistent on partnering with you."

A warmth blossomed in my chest at her words. "That means a lot coming from you, Liv. I know how much this place means to your family."

She nodded, her gaze drifting around the room. "It does. And I'll admit, I was skeptical at first about all these changes. But seeing this..." she gestured to the bustling crowd, the excited chatter filling the air, "I can see that change isn't always a bad thing. You two have created something special here."

Before I could respond, a boisterous group of locals gathered around one of my larger prints and interrupted us. They stared at a panoramic shot of the orchard at sunset with the trees silhouetted against a sky ablaze with color.

"Now that's a view worth framing," Old Man Peters declared, squinting at the image. "Captures the spirit of the place, it does."

Mrs. Johnson nodded in agreement. "Rakel, dear, you have such an eye for beauty. Have you thought about offering photography classes? I bet there'd be quite a bit of interest in the community."

I blinked, surprised by the suggestion. "I hadn't really

considered it, but that's not a bad idea. Maybe a weekend workshop series or something?"

The group enthusiastically supported the idea, and soon I jotted down names of potential students on a spare napkin. As I looked around at the genuine interest and support from my neighbors, I felt a sense of belonging wash over me. This was what I'd been missing in the city with this tight-knit community, this feeling of being truly seen and appreciated for my art.

Throughout the evening, I floated between my gallery space and Tevin's cider tasting area, greeting guests and answering questions about my work. The response was overwhelmingly positive, with several people expressing an interest in commissioning pieces or purchasing prints.

At one point, I found myself in a deep discussion with the owner of the local bookstore about the possibility of hosting a rotating exhibition of my work in their cafe space. The possibilities seemed endless, and I felt a surge of excitement about the future.

As the night wore on, I finally stole a moment alone with Tevin. We snuck out the back door of the barn, escaping to the quiet of the orchard. The crisp night air was a welcome relief after the warmth and bustle inside.

"So," Tevin said, wrapping an arm around my waist as we walked between the rows of bare apple trees. "What do you think? Was it everything you hoped for?"

I leaned into him, feeling a profound sense of contentment. "It was more than I ever dared to hope for," I admitted. "The turnout, the response to my work, the way everyone's embraced our vision, it's kind of overwhelming, in the best possible way."

Tevin pressed a kiss to the top of my head. "You deserve every bit of it, Rakel. Your talent is undeniable, and people are finally getting to see what I've known all along – that you're an incredible artist with a unique perspective."

I felt a lump form in my throat, overcome with emotion. "Thank you," I whispered. "For believing in me, for pushing me to take this leap. I couldn't have done any of this without you."

He stopped walking, turning to face me. In the moonlight, his eyes shone with an intensity that took my breath away. "You're wrong about that," he said softly. "You could have done all of this and more on your own. You're the most talented, determined person I know. I'm just grateful I get to be along for the ride."

I reached up, cupping his face in my hands. "There's no one else I'd rather be on this journey with," I said, before pulling him down for a kiss.

As we broke apart, Tevin's expression turned mischievous. "You know," he said, a hint of excitement in his voice, "tonight isn't the only surprise I had planned."

I raised an eyebrow, intrigued. "Oh really? And what might you be plotting now, Mr. Short?"

He grinned, shaking his head. "Uh-uh, no spoilers. But let's just say I have something special in mind for our six-month anniversary next week. Something that might involve a little adventure outside of Maple Grove."

My curiosity piqued, but I knew better than to try to wheedle more information out of him. Tevin could be surprisingly tight-lipped when he wanted to be. "Well, now you've got me all excited and curious," I pouted playfully.

He laughed, pulling me close again. "Good. A little anticipation never hurt anyone. For now, though, we should probably head back inside before people start to wonder where we've disappeared to."

CHAPTER EIGHT

*R*akel

I smoothed down my dress, taking a deep breath as I surveyed the bustling crowd in our barn. One year. It had been one entire year since Tevin and I had opened the doors to Short & Sweet Ciders and Rakel Boswell Photography. Familiar faces packed the barn, all here to celebrate our success and the community we'd built.

"You okay?" Tevin's voice came from behind me, warm and reassuring as always. I turned to face him, my heart skipping a beat at the sight of him in his tailored suit.

"Just taking it all in," I replied, smiling up at him. "Can you believe it's been a year already?"

He grinned, pulling me close. "Best year of my life," he murmured, pressing a kiss to my forehead.

As we made our way through the crowd, greeting friends and neighbors, I couldn't help but marvel at how far we'd come. The barn looked even more beautiful than it had on opening night, with fairy lights twinkling overhead and the walls adorned with a mix of my latest photographs and vintage apple crates filled with Tevin's newest cider blends.

"Rakel, dear!" Mrs. Johnson called out, waving us over to where she stood with a group of ladies from her book club. "We were just admiring your new autumn collection. The colors are simply breathtaking!"

I beamed at her, feeling a rush of pride. "Thank you so much. I'm glad you like them. How are you enjoying the photography classes?"

Mrs. Johnson's eyes lit up. "Oh, they've been wonderful! Who knew an old gal like me could learn to use one of those fancy digital cameras?"

We chatted for a few more minutes before moving on, making our rounds through the party. Everywhere we went, people congratulated us on our success, praising Tevin's innovative cider flavors and my evolving photography style.

As the evening wore on, I stood by the cider tasting station, sampling Tevin's latest creation of a spiced pear cider that perfectly captured the essence of late autumn.

"What do you think?" Tevin asked, appearing at my side with a nervous energy I couldn't quite place.

I took another sip, savoring the complex flavors. "It's incredible, Tev. You've outdone yourself with this one."

He grinned, but I noticed his hand fidgeting with something in his pocket. Before I could ask what was wrong, he cleared his throat loudly, drawing the attention of everyone nearby.

"Can I have everyone's attention for a moment?" Tevin called out, his voice carrying across the barn. The chatter died down as all eyes turned towards us.

My heart raced. What was he up to?

Tevin took my hand, his palm slightly sweaty, and

turned to face me. "Rakel," he began, his voice thick with emotion, "this past year has been the most amazing adventure of my life. When we opened this place, I thought I couldn't possibly be happier. But every day with you proves me wrong."

Tears pricked at my eyes as he continued, "You've brought so much joy, creativity, and love into my life. You've helped me see the beauty in the everyday moments, just like you capture it in your photographs."

Then, to my utter shock, Tevin dropped on one knee, pulling a small velvet box from his pocket. Gasps and excited murmurs rippled through the crowd.

"Rakel Boswell," Tevin said, his eyes shining with unshed tears, "I can't imagine spending another day without you by my side. Will you marry me?"

He opened the box, revealing a stunning vintage-style ring with a pear-shaped diamond surrounded by smaller stones that caught the light beautifully.

For a moment, I couldn't breathe. I stared at Tevin, then at the ring, then back at his hopeful face. My heart felt like it might burst with happiness.

"Yes," I whispered, then louder, "Yes! Of course, yes!"

The barn erupted in cheers as Tevin slipped the ring onto my finger with shaking hands. He stood up, and I threw my arms around him, kissing him deeply as our friends and family applauded around us.

When we finally broke apart, both of us laughing and crying, well-wishers immediately surrounded us. Liv was the first to reach us, pulling us both into a tight hug.

"Welcome to the family, officially," she said to me, her eyes suspiciously moist. "Though if you ask me, you've been part of it for a while now."

My parents were next, my mom openly weeping as she hugged me tight. "Oh, sweetie," she sniffled, "I'm so happy for you. Your father and I always knew you'd find your place, but this is beyond our wildest dreams."

As the excitement died down and people returned to their conversations, now buzzing with news of our engagement, Tevin pulled me aside to a quiet corner of the barn.

"So," he said, a mischievous glint in his eye, "when should we do this thing?"

I laughed, still feeling giddy. "Well, I've always loved the idea of a summer wedding. What do you think about the first of summer, right here in the barn?"

Tevin's face lit up. "That sounds perfect. And I think I know just the photographer for the job," he added with a wink.

The next few months flew by in a whirlwind of wedding planning, cider brewing, and photoshoots. We kept things relatively simple, wanting our wedding to reflect the rustic charm of the orchard and the barn that had brought us together.

I threw myself into the details, determined to create the perfect day. We chose a color scheme of soft peach and sage green, echoing the colors of the orchard in early summer. I spent hours scouring antique shops and flea markets for vintage apple crates and mason jars to use as decorations.

Tevin, ever the innovator, insisted on creating a special cider blend just for our wedding. He spent weeks experimenting with different flavor combinations, driving Liv slightly mad at his constant requests for taste tests.

Before we knew it, the big day had arrived. I woke up early on the morning of our wedding, my stomach fluttering with a mix of excitement and nerves. I'd spent the night at my old apartment above my studio in town, following the tradition of not seeing the groom before the wedding.

A knock at the door interrupted my reverie. "Rakel? You up, honey?" my mom called out.

"Come in!" I replied, grinning as she entered, followed by Liv and my best friend, Sarah.

"Ready to get beautified?" Sarah asked, holding up a large makeup bag.

The next few hours passed in a blur of hairstyling, makeup application, and nervous laughter. As I slipped into the vintage-inspired lace gown with cap sleeves and an open back, a sense of calm settled over me.

"Oh, Rakel," my mom gasped, her eyes filling with tears. "You look absolutely beautiful."

Liv nodded in agreement, handing me a small box. "Something borrowed," she said with a smile. "It was our mom's favorite bracelet. I thought you might like to wear it today."

I hugged her tightly, touched by the gesture. "Thank you, Liv. It's perfect."

As we made our way to the orchard, I felt a growing sense of anticipation. We'd had the ceremony outside among the apple trees in the grove of late blossoms, with the reception to follow in the barn.

The orchard looked like something out of a fairytale. Rows of white chairs faced an arch made of twisted apple branches, adorned with delicate peach and white flowers. Mason jars filled with wildflowers hung from the trees, swaying gently in the warm summer breeze.

I took a deep breath, clutching my bouquet of peonies and garden roses as I prepared to walk down the aisle. My dad appeared at my side, looking dashing in his suit and barely containing his emotions.

"Ready, pumpkin?" he asked, offering me his arm.

I nodded, unable to speak past the lump in my throat. As the music started and we began our walk, I scanned the crowd of familiar faces. Mrs. Johnson was dabbing at her eyes with a handkerchief, while Old Man Peters looked uncharacteristically misty-eyed.

And then I saw Tevin, standing at the end of the aisle, looking so handsome it took my breath away. His eyes locked with mine, and suddenly, everything else faded away. It was just us, in this perfect moment.

The ceremony passed in a blur of emotion. We'd written our own vows, and I struggled to get through mine without breaking down completely.

"Tevin," I began, my voice shaky, "you came into my life when I least expected it, but exactly when I needed you most. You saw the beauty in my work when I was doubting myself, and you've encouraged me every step of the way. You're my partner in every sense of the word, in business, in creativity, and in life. I promise to always support your dreams, to be your biggest cheerleader, and to love you unconditionally. I can't wait to see what adventures we'll have together."

Tevin's vows were equally heartfelt, bringing tears to my eyes and laughter to my lips as he recounted our first meeting at the farmer's market and how he'd known even then that I was someone special.

As we exchanged rings and were pronounced husband and wife, the orchard erupted in cheers and applause. Tevin pulled me close for our first kiss as a married couple, and I felt my heart soar with happiness.

The reception that followed was everything we'd hoped for and more. The barn looked magical, with strings of lights crisscrossing the ceiling and long tables decorated with lace runners, vintage apple crates filled with flowers, and candles in mason jars.

Tevin's special wedding cider was a hit with its light floral notes perfectly complementing the summer evening.

We danced our first dance to an acoustic version of *Sweet Disposition*, laughing as Tevin tried (and failed) to twirl me without stepping on my dress.

As the night wore on and our guests enjoyed the feast of locally sourced foods we'd chosen, I took mental snapshots of the moments around me. Liv gave a heartfelt toast that had us all in stitches one moment and teary-eyed the next. My dad attempted to do the Electric Slide. Mrs. Johnson taught a group of younger guests how to do a traditional barn dance.

Tevin found me by the dessert table, sneaking a bite of our apple cider donut cake. "Having fun, Mrs. Short?" he asked, wrapping an arm around my waist.

I grinned up at him, still getting used to my new name. "The best time, Mr. Short. Though I have to say, I'm looking forward to some alone time with my new husband."

He waggled his eyebrows suggestively. "Oh really? And what did you have in mind?"

Before I could respond, a group of Tevin's cousins interrupted us insisting we join them on the dance floor. As the crowd pulled us in, laughing and swaying to the music, I caught Tevin's eye.

In that moment, surrounded by our loved ones in the place that had brought us together, I felt an overwhelming sense of gratitude and joy. Whatever challenges life might throw our way, I knew we'd face them together, just as we had this past year.

As the night drew to a close and our guests departed, Tevin and I snuck away for a quiet moment alone. We wandered hand in hand through the orchard, the sounds of the party fading behind us.

"So," Tevin said, pulling me close, "was it everything you dreamed of?"

I looked up at him, at the man who had become my

partner in every sense of the word, and felt my heart swell with love. "It was more than I ever dared to dream," I replied softly. "But then again, that's kind of our thing, isn't it? Exceeding expectations?"

Tevin laughed, leaning down to kiss me tenderly. As we stood there in the orchard, the stars twinkling overhead and the promise of our future stretching out before us, I knew that this was just the beginning of our greatest adventure yet.

Read the next book Bunches of Passion.

ABOUT ANN LAUREL

Ann loves writing about life and issues Christian couples face, all with a big dose of romance.

Sign up for Ann's newsletter.

Printed in Dunstable, United Kingdom